Illustrations by Isabel Muñoz

Written by Elena Ferrari

Designed by Nick Ackland

White Star Kids® is a registered trademark property of White Star s.r.l.

© 2020 White Star s.r.l.
Piazzale Luigi Cadorna, 6
20123 Milan, Italy
www.whitestar.it

Produced by I am a bookworm.

Translation: Iceigeo, Milan (Katherine Clifton)
Editing: Michele Suchomel-Casey

All rights reserved. No part of this publication may be reproduced, stored in
a retrieval system or transmitted in any form or by any means, electronic,
mechanical, photocopying, recording or otherwise, without written permission
from the publisher.

ISBN 978-88-544-1621-5
1 2 3 4 5 6   24 23 22 21 20

Printed in Italy by Rotolito S.p.A. - Seggiano di Pioltello (Milan)

8/23
4–

The life of
Louis
Pasteur

WSkids
WHITE STAR KIDS

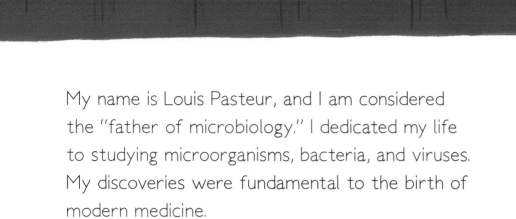

My name is Louis Pasteur, and I am considered
the "father of microbiology." I dedicated my life
to studying microorganisms, bacteria, and viruses.
My discoveries were fundamental to the birth of
modern medicine.

Come with me on the fascinating voyage that led
me to invent the first vaccine and to defeat a number
of terrible diseases.

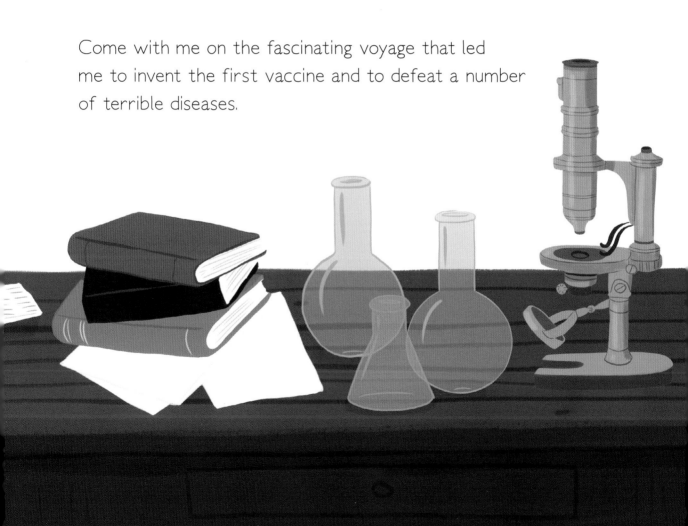

I was born on December 27, 1822, in Dole, in the Jura Mountains of eastern France. The region is now called Bourgogne-Franche-Comté, and it is quite close to the Swiss border. My family was not wealthy; my father, Jean Pasteur, was a leather tanner and a veteran of the Napoleonic Wars. I was one of five children.

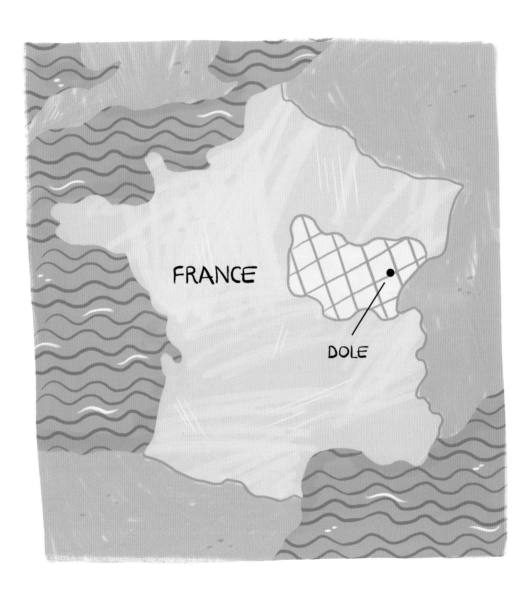

Jeanne

Jean

Louis

Jean
Denis

Virginie

Josephine

Emilie

I began my studies in the town of Arbois and went to secondary school at the Royal College of Besançon, where I was awarded a diploma in Science in 1842.

Afterward, I enrolled at the university in Paris. When the faculty president discovered that I was a brilliant student, he suggested that I apply to Paris's prestigious École Normale Supérieure.

I was admitted to the examinations in fourteenth place, but I was not satisfied with this result and decided to work harder. The following year I took third place. In 1847, I attained my doctorate by writing two dissertations: one in chemistry about the saturation capacity of arsenious acid, and one in physics about the study of phenomena relating to the circular polarization of liquids.

ICI FVT
LE LABORATOIRE
DE
PASTEUR

My work and my studies are closely linked to the École Normale Supérieure in Paris, the prestigious university where a research laboratory bears my name.

After my doctorate, I dedicated much of my time to analyzing the form and properties of crystals in tartaric acid, which forms during the fermentation of wine.

My research was fundamental for the development of stereochemistry, which studies the structure of molecules and their properties and is still very important in the field of pharmaceuticals.

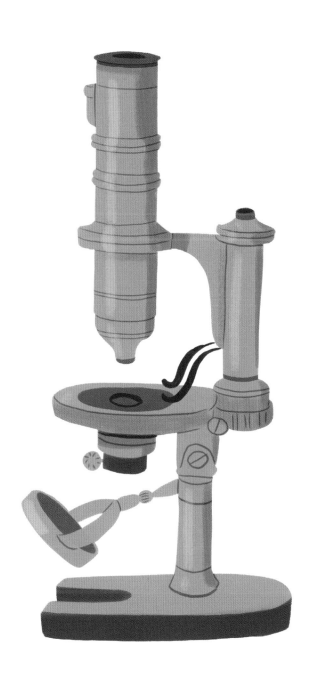

Soon after this (less than two years later!), I became a professor of chemistry at the University of Strasbourg. There, I met Marie Laurent, the daughter of the rector of the university.

I fell in love with her, and we were married that same year, 1849.
Marie was also very interested in chemistry, and in the evenings,
she helped me with my studies. My wife was not only my companion
for life; she was also my cherished assistant.

We had five children, but tragically three of them died of typhoid fever when they were still very young. The loss of my children was one of the reasons I spent so many years seeking a cure for infectious diseases.

CAMILLE

JEANNE

CECILE

When we moved to Lille in 1854, I began studying alcoholic fermentations; in particular, I analyzed the process of transforming must (the juice of grapes) into wine. I continued these studies even after I went to work at the École Normale Supérieure as the director of scientific studies three years later. I began working in this field after a number of wine producers asked me why their wine sometimes became acidic and undrinkable before being bottled.

Generally, wine was made by adding yeasts to the must and leaving it to ferment for a few weeks. Before I began studying the process, no one had analyzed what happens during that period of time.

I analyzed the process and found that the fermentation, that is, "life in the absence of oxygen," was linked to the development of particular cells, which I called "ferments" and are now known as "yeasts."

At that time, it was thought that products went bad or sour because of microorganisms that formed spontaneously inside them. This theory was called spontaneous generation. In 1861, after observing yeasts, I was able to demonstrate that life is always generated by living microorganisms that multiply repeatedly.

Now, all I had to do was find a way to eliminate the bacteria that spoiled the wine. In 1862, after a number of experiments, I discovered a way of killing many bacteria by heating liquids (wine, beer, milk) to about 140°F (60°C) before they were bottled. This system is still used today for sterilizing foods. The process is called pasteurization in my honor.

These discoveries made me famous. In the years that followed, I continued my studies, calling many brilliant young scientists to work in my laboratories. They helped me when my studies were impeded after I suffered a severe stroke in 1864.

I was hindered in the latter part of my life by these physical problems, but the experiments I carried out were extremely important for medicine. In particular, they were important in fighting infectious diseases, which were—and to some extent still are—the main causes of death throughout human history.

Finally, in 1879, we found a way to weaken bacteria and immunize animals and human beings from a number of diseases. We concentrated our studies on one specific disease transmitted by animals that affected many victims: rabies.

In 1885, in cooperation with my assistant Émile Roux, we tested an anti-rabies vaccine on a human being. A nine-year-old child arrived at my laboratory with his mother; he had been bitten by a rabid dog. His name was Joseph Meister, and he was afraid of injections.

In order to convince him that there was nothing to fear, I showed him the effects of rabies on animals. The child was very afraid, but he courageously agreed to the treatment. Thanks to this vaccine, he did not die and he did not contract rabies.

A few months later, on March 1, 1886, I reported to the Academy of Sciences that I had vaccinated 350 people, all bitten by rabid dogs, who would almost certainly have become ill. I was able to state that there was only one death and that 349 people survived. At last, it was possible to say that rabies had been overcome.

ANTI-RABIES
VACCINE

In 1887, thanks to an international donation, I founded an important research institute in Paris, where Joseph Meister, the first child I saved from rabies, worked.

INSTITUT PASTEUR
CHIMIE BIOLOGIQUE

When I died in 1895 at Marnes-la-Coquette, after a stroke, I was buried at the institute that still bears my name.

Throughout my life, I studied infinitely tiny creatures that no one even knew existed. My intuition and my perseverance allowed me to save millions of lives.

Never neglect details, be persistent, and you will attain great results.

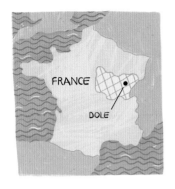

Louis Pasteur is born
in Dole, France,
on December 27.

He earns a doctorate
in chemistry and
physics.

1822

1847

1842

He earns bachelor
degrees in science.

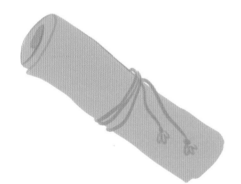

He begins studying alcoholic fermentations.

1854

1849

He marries Marie Laurent.

1861

He rejects the theory of spontaneous generation.

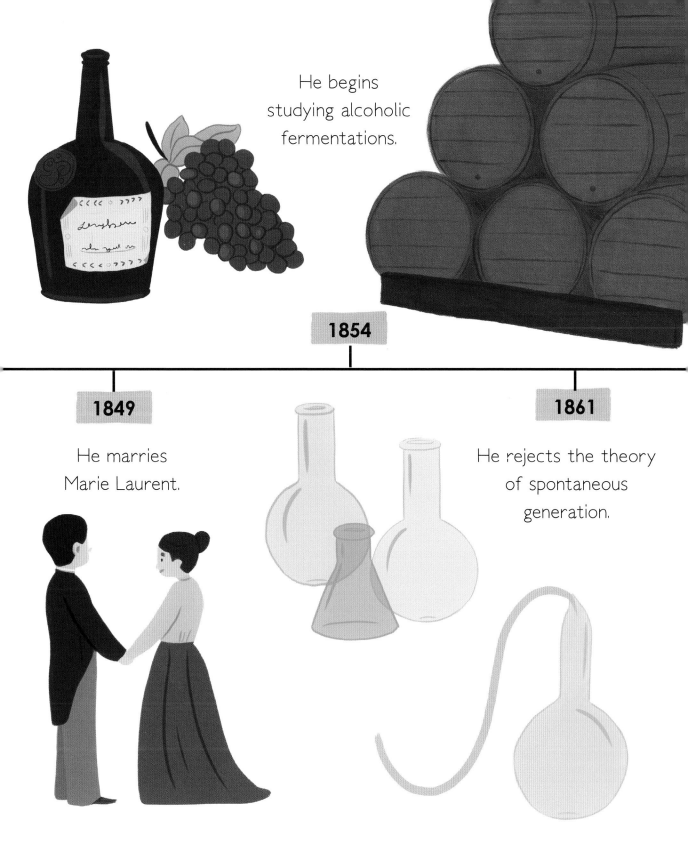

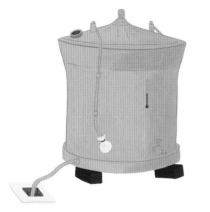

He invents the process known as pasteurization.

Pasteur discovers the concept of immunization.

1862

1879

1864

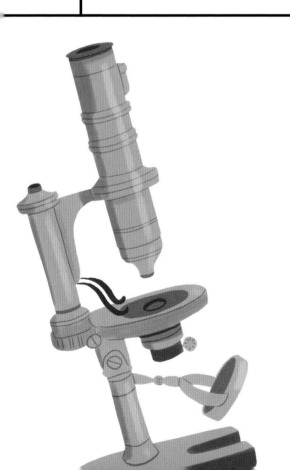

He suffers a stroke.

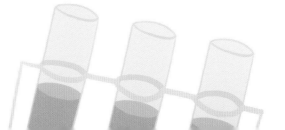

He founds a research institute that still carries his name.

INSTITUT PASTEUR
CHIMIE BIOLOGIQUE

1887

1885

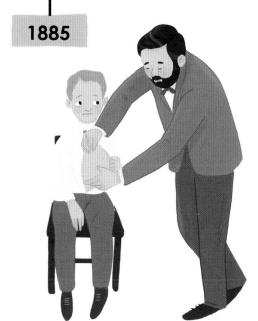

Pasteur tries an anti-rabies vaccine on a human being for the first time.

1895

He dies at Marnes-la-Coquette from a stroke.

QUESTIONS

Q1. In which city did Pasteur begin his studies?

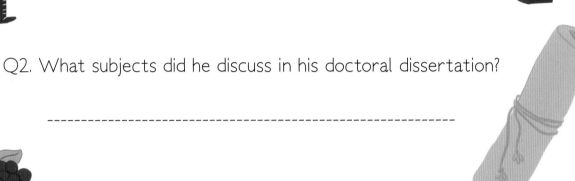

Q2. What subjects did he discuss in his doctoral dissertation?

Q3. What did he begin to analyze
after his doctorate?

Q4. What was the name of Pasteur's wife?

Q5. When did he begin studying fermentation?

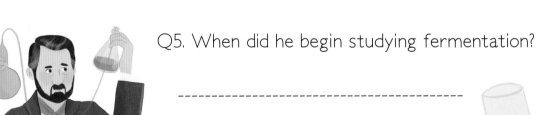

Q6. What is the name of the method
that Pasteur invented in 1862?

_____

Q7. How is rabies transmitted?

_____

Q8. Who was the first child vaccinated
against rabies?

_____

Q9. What did Pasteur found in 1887?

_____

Q10. Where did Pasteur die?

_____

ANSWERS

A1. In Arbois.

A2. Chemistry and physics.

A3. The form and properties of tartaric acid.

A4. Marie Laurent.

A5. In 1854.

A6. Pasteurization.

A7. By bites from rabid animals.

A8. Joseph Meister.

A9. A research institute.

10. In Marnes-la-Coquette, France.